First Little Readers™

# Too Many Unicorns

by Liza Charlesworth

ISBN: 978-1-338-29800-0

Illustrated by Tammie Lyon

First printing, June 2018.

 Published by Scholastic Inc. Printed in Jiaxing, China.

Once upon a time,
there was a unicorn
named Sue.

She had a horn.
She had wings.
She had a rainbow tail.

Sue lived in Animal Land.
She was friends with a cow
and a dog and a bear.

But Sue was the one
and only unicorn.
That made her feel sad.

One day Sue saw an ad
for a place called Unicorn Land.
"I must go!" she said.

Sue said good-bye
to her friends.
Then off she flew!

Things were different
in Unicorn Land.
At first, Sue felt happy.

Sue saw unicorns at the mall.
Unicorns, unicorns, unicorns!

Sue saw unicorns at the lake.
Unicorns, unicorns, unicorns!

Sue saw unicorns at the fair.
Unicorns, unicorns, unicorns!

Guess what?
There were just
too many unicorns!
So Sue felt sad.

What did Sue do?
She left Unicorn Land
and flew back home.

Guess what?
Sue was the one
and only unicorn again.

But now Sue felt happy.
She was different.
She was special!

Then the unicorn named Sue
and her friends
lived happily ever after!